HOW MUCH CAN I SEE?

A Novel in Essays

Volume I

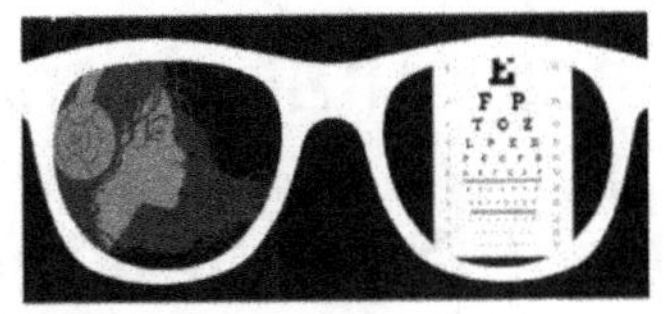

By:

M. L. FARRELL

First Electronic Edition: April 2022

First Print Edition: April 2022

LETLOVEGLOW
AUTHOR SERVICES
BY D. D. SCOTT

PRAISE FOR M. L. FARRELL:

"M. L. Farrell's debut book is an incredible opportunity to learn the challenges faced, the victories won, and the battles lost during the heart-expanding journey of living life legally blind. Poignant, but with a wonderful sense of humor woven in, she has written a story you'll never forget. I'm looking forward to her next book!"

D. D. Scott

International Bestselling Author

I would like to dedicate my book to my family members who are no longer here with me. I would like to give a special dedication to my grandmother, Mary Farrell. I think she would be proud to see me writing this. I would also like to give a special dedication to my sweet girl, Penny. She wasn't just a dog … she was a member of the family.

CONTENTS

PROLOGUE

"Goin' Up Yonder"

(Tramaine Hawkins)

1

CHAPTER ONE

"ER"

5

CHAPTER TWO

"Cinderella"

25

CHAPTER THREE

The N-Word

33

CHAPTER FOUR

"The Fairly OddParents"

39

CHAPTER FIVE

"Girl"

(Destiny's Child)

47

CHAPTER SIX

"When You Believe"

(Mariah Carey & Whitney Houston)

53

CHAPTER SEVEN

Arkansas Regrets

63

CHAPTER EIGHT

"Chasing Cars"

(Snow Patrol)

71

CHAPTER NINE

My Mom's Strength

79

CHAPTER TEN

"Grey's Anatomy"

83

CHAPTER ELEVEN

"A New Day Has Come"

(Celine Deion)

95

CHAPTER TWELVE

"Take Me to the King"

(Tamela Mann)

103

CHAPTER THIRTEEN

"Beautiful"

(Christina Aguilera)

113

CHAPTER FOURTEEN

"Never Would Have Made It"

(Marvin Sapp)

119

EPILOGUE

"Wings"

(Little Mix)

Rain Drops Make Puddles

125

ACKNOWLEDGEMENTS

128

NOTE FROM THE AUTHOR
129

ABOUT THE AUTHOR
131

BOOKS BY THE AUTHOR
133

PROLOGUE

"Goin' Up Yonder"

(Tramaine Hawkins)

"It's okay that you broke up, Maya, but you've got to wake up."

I was so confused. Why did I have to wake up? It was just me and my grandmother on my uncle's couch.

"You need to wake up now."

"But we're watching TV, Grandma. We're sitting on the couch."

There was so much peace, sitting in my uncle's house, next to my grandmother, just the two of us, watching all her favorite home improvement shows.

But then the next commercial would come on, and my grandmother would start another conversation with me, the topic always the same.

"Oh well, you know," Grandma said, "it's okay that you've broken up. But you need to wake up now. It's okay that things didn't quite work out your way."

"Grandma, what do you mean? We're sitting here, watching TV. I am awake," I said, getting more confused and more frustrated each time we repeated this exchange.

"Maya, you NEED to wake up now!"

Suddenly, I jerked awake. And I realized I was strapped to a hospital bed.

What was happening? And how had I been on my uncle's couch just moments ago, talking to my grandmother, when she had been dead for over six months?

M. L. Farrell

As God gives me grace

I'll run this race

Until I see my Saviour

Face to face

~ ~ *"Goin Up Yonder"*

(Tramaine Hawkins)

CHAPTER ONE
"ER"

That person strapped to that hospital bed in ICU was me – Maya Farris.

I'm 30 years old, and I am legally blind. But just because I'm legally blind doesn't mean everything in my life has been tragic.

My life has been a little *Cinderella* … but it's been a lot more *Gilmore Girls*.

When you're legally blind, TV is your escape. Well, TV and music. So, you'll have to excuse me for sharing my story as if each chapter of my life is either a TV show or a song, or both. And each person involved is a main character or a side kick or the reason a particular song stays on my favorite playlists.

As for the villains?

Well, I really don't believe in villains. My grandmother used to tell me that God brings people in and out of your life, and if you need to remove them and won't, God will. So, yeah, God's removed a few characters for me. But not until I learned what they were here to teach me, and I'm grateful for every lesson.

But back to my ICU hospital bed …

For as long as I can remember, I have been sick, and I don't mean like a cough or cold sick, I mean, when I was about five years old, I was diagnosed with cancer, Embryonic rhabdomyosarcoma to be exact, and that changed my life forever. And it came at a time in my life when I was transitioning from living with my mother to living with my grandfather. I was too young to understand what was going on with that transition, but I did understand that I wasn't going to be living with my mother and brothers anymore.

I remember being in the 1st grade, and I was so sick. I kept having to go to the nurse's office. One day, I went to her office, she felt my head, and I had the worst fever ever! She called my grandfather and sent me home, and I slept for most of that afternoon, but when I woke up, I was off kilter, wobbling around and miserable. I went downstairs (because that's where my grandfather's room was), and my uncle Lance was trying to give me some kind of medicine. Looking back on it, it was the sweetest thing in the world because he was only in the 5th grade at the time.

Soon after taking the medicine, I began throwing it up all over him, so I was taken to the ER, where they told my grandfather that I needed an emergency appendectomy. When they removed my appendix, they found a tumor.

What makes the situation even more crazy was that, at the time, my grandfather didn't believe I was sick. He thought I was faking it because of everything going on in my life regarding my custody case. I didn't really understand what losing my vision meant until I returned to school, and I couldn't participate with the other kids. There was so much I couldn't do. There was special equipment I needed to use which brought a lot of attention on me that I didn't want, and that's when the bullying began. The other kids just didn't really understand what was going on with me.

Despite the bullying, it didn't take me long to realize that my classmates liked to sit behind me because the print on my papers was so much bigger than what was on theirs', which meant they could see my answers. Since I couldn't do a lot of other things, I focused on my schooling, making sure it was good. So, yeah, they were copying from the right kid.

I didn't have a lot of genuine friends. I didn't have anyone who would play with me. I got picked last for a lot of things or just not acknowledged at all. But I ended up making one friend, whose name was

How Much Can I See?

Destiny, and she became my best friend for a really long time. She lived around the corner from me, and she always included me. I was over at her house all the time. She made me feel like a person, even though I was struggling.

When I got into middle school, I ended up with another friend who made me feel the same way. She would invite me to her house for sleepovers. We would hang out. She came to my house for sleepovers. It was nice … so nice to be acknowledged.

After 6th grade, though, things got even crazier. I wanted to go live with my mom. So, I packed all my stuff and did that for the summer. She was living in Arkansas, and she enrolled me in the Arkansas School for the Blind. Things were so good for a while.

But then, my grandfather wanted me back, and he showed up in Arkansas, with the police, to take me back. And I had to go. It was so hard for me, and I cried the whole way home. After I got home, I spent a lot of time being angry at him, even though I knew he truly wanted to help his daughter (my mom) and me and be our hero.

That's when I decided I wanted to go to a blind school in Indianapolis. Because we lived far enough away from the school, I could live on campus and only have to go home to my grandfather's house on weekends and holidays.

How Much Can I See?

I found so much acceptance at my new blind school. I learned a lot about being capable. I could do things I never thought possible for me, with modifications. Of course, I also made friends there, which was great. And I was able to remain there until the end of my freshman year, when I moved back to Arkansas because I wanted to live with my mom so desperately, not knowing that things with her weren't as sunny as I had thought.

I had a little brother who was stealing. My older brother was very, very angry. And my mom was struggling. So, when I got there, there were times when we didn't have lights, and I had never experienced that before. There were times when we had to stay with other people, outside our family, which I had also never experienced before.

But, overall, it was great, because I also got to go to the blind school there, part-time. And because of my brothers, I also got to experience public school, and make friends there.

Being back in Arkansas, despite the challenges, changed my life for the better. I still had lots of surgeries – a couple of eye surgeries and bowel obstruction procedures. But that was pretty much my norm.

How Much Can I See?

People assume that because you've had cancer and survived, your life is rainbows, but that's not the case.

In 2012, we left Arkansas, for two reasons: one, I wanted to go back to Indiana because the state offered so many options for the blind; and two, my mom was engaged.

My mom was a nurse and had her license changed to Indiana. But there were some issues with that, which meant she wasn't able to work for a while, so she had to rely on her fiancé for money. Problem was, he would only give her $40 for groceries for our entire house, while he was gambling … and gambling heavy. He also wasn't paying the bills, and we got an eviction notice. That was crazy!

I reconnected with some people from my past in Indiana, but I wasn't into partying. I wanted to do something more fulfilling in my life. But, for a couple of years, I was just kind of lost, trying to figure out what I wanted. My health also took a turn. And not for the better. The doctors thought I had a respiratory infection, but despite their best efforts, I wasn't healing. I was throwing up all the time, and I spent a lot of time in the Emergency Room.

By January 2014, we had a ton of snow, and it was minus 14 degrees. Our power went out. We had to go to our neighbor's house. And I was so sooo sick!

My mom wanted me to go with her to Anderson, where she had met the man who is now my stepfather, but I wanted to stay in Indianapolis with my boyfriend.

I ended up in the Emergency Room multiple times, where I met a nurse named Abby, who called a doctor explaining how many times I'd recently been in there. My blood pressure was outrageous, and they admitted me on January 22nd for an ileus (a bowel blockage in the intestines). Surgery was done right before Valentine's Day, and I did feel better for about two days. They were talking about sending me home, but the night before I was to go home, the vomiting began again, and it was black and tar-like (which I later found out was fecal matter).

They put a tube down my throat to pump my stomach. They figured out that when they removed the ileus, another piece of the original obstruction had migrated, so that piece now had to be removed, as well. The procedure left me with a post-op infection, and for the first time, I experienced a wound vac, which was nuts. I spent a lot of time in the ICU and then the PCU, and that was a period of time I don't remember much because I had such a high fever. I was hallucinating a lot. It was honestly terrifying. I had never been so afraid in my life.

I got out of the hospital in March of that year, but I was only out a few days before I was in a large amount of pain. They told me I had a cyst on my ovaries. At that time, they wanted to operate, but the doctors decided another surgery in that short of a time frame could mean that I could die, so they didn't remove the ovarian cyst. Insane, I know.

Finally out of the hospital, I wanted to dive into this program in Indianapolis called Indypendence Job Corps, which I had been wanting to do for a long time. In June 2014, I began the program, and I graduated six months later. Just a couple of weeks after my graduation, I got a job!

Lowe's Company, Inc. was excellent about making sure I had the technology I needed to do my job, and I met some really great people, but as always, I still had health issues, which caused me to be away from work ... a lot. I worked for almost a year, but got sick again, and had another surgery (February 2016) for a massive hernia and bowel issue. After that surgery, I had additional problems with my eyes and had another eye surgery. In 2017, I began vomiting again, which was diagnosed as chronic pain due to all the medical procedures I'd endured. It was something I really had to wrap my mind around. *Am I ever going to be healthy?*

It was 2018 when my grandmother started getting really sick. She was in and out of the hospital several times. She had told my aunt that she didn't think she was going to make it to Thanksgiving that year, so she spent two months with us in Indiana, sharing her recipes and sharing her love. She passed away around Thanksgiving, as she had told us she would.

Losing her was really really difficult for me. It was my grandmother who helped me through the breakup I was going through with my boyfriend of five years as well as the miscarriage we had recently been through.

It was just back-to-back trauma that year. So, it's no surprise that I ended up horribly sick, again.

Fast forward to mid-2019, and that's why you were introduced to me first in yet another hospital bed, this time strapped to it, with my grandmother's beautiful spirit from beyond encouraging me to wake up and rejoin the land of the living.

CHAPTER TWO

"Cinderella"

Now that you know my medical story, I want to share how all this felt to me.

I had so much trauma as a kid. Going from being able to play to constantly needing help with everything just to live my life. I think the hardest part was the bullying, and not just from other people, but from my family.

My uncles and their friends always asking me, 'How many fingers am I holding up?' Making jokes about something I didn't even understand. I had to brush that off all the time, but it was so painful. I felt like I didn't have peace anywhere. Not at school. Not at home. I was just hurting.

Boys didn't like me. Girls only liked me when they wanted to hook up with my uncles. My relationships with my brothers weren't sibling relationships because we didn't know each other that way. We just knew each other and sometimes lived together. My grandfather was there, but he was absent a great deal as he worked hard to provide for all of us. His wife ran the house. And that's when I became Cinderella.

At times, it felt as if everyone benefited from being there … except me. They got my disability payments, and my mother was able to finish nursing school because she didn't have to take care of me. It was so hard, for all of us. Back then, I didn't understand disability, and that my grandfather and his wife were receiving the payments. All I knew is that I felt like a burden.

Britney, my grandfather's wife, would say things like, 'We're spending our money taking care of you, and you need so much help … you're really expensive'.

I think perhaps she was just overwhelmed. I sincerely believe she wanted to help by agreeing with her husband, my grandfather, to take me in. And maybe … because I wasn't a perfect little girl, but was one incredibly sick child, it was much more difficult than she expected. Whatever the reason, it was hard to live with someone who often made you feel like she didn't want you there.

And my grandfather just wasn't present that much. (Mind you, he wasn't present, not because he didn't care, but because he was forever and always working, trying to provide for us and be our hero.) I just couldn't grasp why they would fight so hard to keep a kid they didn't seem to want.

I remember they remodeled my room once, buying me all new furniture. And I remember feeling as if they did that as a way to keep me in the house after the court battles for custody started.

Was I nothing more than an extra check in the mail? That's what I often wondered, no matter who I was living with.

During that difficult time, my favorite thing was going to my grandmother's house in Arkansas. I got to be around my cousins. I got to be a kid. And I got to feel loved and wanted. No child in the world wants to feel like they're not loved and not wanted.

And I'm not saying that my family in Indiana didn't help me. They taught me extreme survival things, things I needed to learn, like how to cross a busy street as a blind person. And they were the ones who shuttled me to all my doctors' appointments and treatments. But in all other ways, when my grandmother left for Arkansas, I felt abandoned.

I know that my mom left to get a better job, but she left me behind. She took my brothers, but she left me. And I felt very, very abandoned.

That's when I started acting out. Because I just didn't care. It's hard to grow up thinking no one wants you. That you're nothing but a burden. And that transferred into some of my negative behaviors. But I own that.

The trauma of constant surgeries was also very hard. People were supportive, but no one wants to be the blind kid. The sick kid. And the black kid.

I felt like I was always disappointing someone. Even after I moved out of my grandfather's house, my mom still had to figure out how to deal with a kid with disabilities. My brothers had to learn how to live with a sister with disabilities.

Those things were just really really hard. For all of us. And they required major lifestyle adjustments. And they required hard choices.

But I'll say it again here (as I will throughout my story):

I don't believe in villains.
God brings people in and out
of your life, and if you need
to remove them and won't,
God will.

So, yeah, God's removed a few of the characters I'm sharing with you. But not until I learned what they were here to teach me, and I'm grateful for every lesson.

CHAPTER THREE
The N-Word

When I was a child, there was a moment when I felt like Lance and Leo, my grandfather's sons with Britney, were my actual siblings, and it was because a white kid called me the N-word on the bus.

It was one of the times when we were all in school together. I was in the 1st grade, Leo was in 2nd grade, and Lance was in the

5th grade. Actually, it was the only time we were all in school together.

This kid called me the N-word on the bus. Lance and Leo had someone walk me home from the bus, so I got their safely, and they stayed on the bus, getting at the kid's stop, where they beat him up pretty good.

The kid's dad came over to my grandfather's house later that night and told him that his sons had beat up his son.

"Well, your son called my kids the N-word on the bus. Why do you think that's okay?" my grandfather asked the man.

The man had no answer for that and left.

That was a period of time where both Lance and Leo were more like siblings to me. And it was weird, as I was always in the background of their lives, and they were always in the background of mine. But I had cancer. I was in the hospital and sick a lot. Meanwhile, they still got to live their childhoods, so we didn't really get to know each other. But it didn't matter on that day. They were there for me when I needed them.

From time to time, girls would befriend me, only so they could get to know Lance and Leo, and that was hard for me. I never knew who really wanted to be friends with me versus who wanted to befriend me only to get to them.

Lance and I got closer just before I moved to Arkansas with my mom, sometime between 2006 and 2007. He had just gotten his license, and I was going to the blind school in Indianapolis, so sometimes, on Sundays, he would take me back and forth when I wasn't staying with relatives or friends. (I stayed with other people a lot, so I didn't have to go home during the custody battle.)

As for Leo, well … it was like everyone just knew me as his little sister, even though, we always corrected them and told them that I was actually his niece.

There's not much else to say about my relationships with them. It was usually just

How Much Can I See?

a distant sibling kind of situation … except for that one big day on the bus.

CHAPTER FOUR

"The Fairly OddParents"

I had just finished the 7th grade, and it was the summertime. I went to my grandmother's house, and everyone was there – my Uncle Keith and all his kids, Aunt Keera and her kids, some of my cousins, and my grandma. It was a really big deal. My mom was home from Arkansas, too.

And it was really awesome! We had a really good time!

I found out that my grandfather had told my mom that I could finally go and live with her. I was going to spend the summer with her in Arkansas. So, I was really excited! Living apart from her had been really difficult.

So, that summer was pretty good. I got to hang out with my brothers and get to know them. And then my mom ended up enrolling me in the blind school the beginning of my 8th grade year. I met some people and was finding my footing. I even joined the track team.

But my grandfather wasn't happy. He was worried about me. Since I was living with my mom again, my social security income ended up going to her. And even though he knew that would help her take care of me, he also knew how hard it had to be, as the single mom she was at the time, to provide for me, as well as my brothers.

I remember one day my grandfather called, and he was angry because he didn't know where my mom lived or worked or anything else about how we were living. My oldest brother told him to just leave us alone because I was happy. She's at the blind school, he told him. She's enjoying life. Just leave us alone and let her be happy.

A few days later, I had an eye doctor appointment, and then I was going back to school and then on to a track meet. I got to school late, but I had a note from my doctor. So, all was good there. But only a few minutes after I got to class, I was sent to the office.

What was happening was that my grandfather showed up at my school with a police officer, and he said that my mom had kidnapped me and that I was supposed to be living with him. She needed to relinquish me into his custody, according to him.

How Much Can I See?

The school wouldn't allow him entrance, but I ended up having to leave anyway, as my mom couldn't prove she was supposed to have me till December when we were to go to court in Indiana for another custody hearing.

That was such a horrible moment for me. I cried so hard! My relationship with my grandfather was never the same after that. I cried all the way back to Indiana. And I cried for days after that.

I know now how much he wanted to help me, and my mom. And I know, deep down, that he thought only he could take care of me the way he felt I needed to be taken care of. But I sure didn't recognize or feel that way back then when it was happening.

I think I only went to public school for two weeks before I ended up back at the blind school. *If he wanted me so bad, why did he ship me off to the Indiana blind school so quickly after getting me back?* And yes, I did thrive at blind schools, but it just wasn't the same. I wanted to be where my mom was ... where my brothers and grandmother were.

My mom would drive to Indiana from Arkansas to attend what she could at my school and be a part of my life. But I grew to hate my grandfather, whether or not that was fair. If I'm being honest, that's how I felt. For him to rip me away from my mother and my family and friends, just to ship me off somewhere else, was just a horrible, horrible thing for me to try and understand. It hurt in a way I just can't explain.

As a child, and as a child with so much trauma because of my health, or lack thereof, being tossed around in my mother and grandfather's custody battle was rough. And even though I knew they all wanted what they felt was best for me, what about how it felt for me, being in the middle of all that?

That custody case shaped me a whole lot. It molded me.

After that, I carried around a lot of anger and a lot of hurt.

I felt like just a paycheck to the current winner. No one could collect a check on a child that didn't live with them. And it was hard growing up in a house, whichever one I was in at the time, wondering if I was loved for me or for the check that came with taking care of me. When you grow up like that, it causes you to have a lot of insecurities. It's a trauma that's really hard to heal from, and one I work to heal from every single day as an adult.

CHAPTER FIVE

"Girl"
(Destiny's Child)

There are parts of my life that have really defined me. And a lot of parts of my life have shaped me. A lot of parts have also helped me grow. But everything that's happened to me isn't always a tragic defining moment.

For example, my goddaughter's mom has been one of my closest friends since I met her many, many years ago, before I started to go to the blind school in Indianapolis full-time. I used to go to summer camp at the school, and I met many of the people who attended there full-time. One of the people I met was my goddaughter's mom. Over the years, our relationship has been rocky, but it's always stayed strong.

Shortly after my mom had to send me back to my grandfather's, I got really sick. I ended up having a bowel obstruction and spent a couple of weeks in the hospital. It was rough, and I missed a lot of school.

A lot of people called and checked on me. However, my goddaughter's mom showed me true friendship. She asked her mom to take her to the hospital, and she sat there with me for hours upon hours. She knitted me a scarf – a pink and blue scarf that I loved. And she also brought me a purse that was gray said "Brat" on it in purple rhinestones, which was perfect!

That was the day I learned what real friendship looked like. A lot of people claimed to be my friend, but even though they could have come to see me at the hospital, they didn't.

That said, I wasn't always the best friend, either. I was young and stupid. But not my goddaughter's mother. She always showed me kindness, and she was always and consistently there for me. When I needed her, she showed up – she showed up at the hospital, she sat with me, she got to know me better. Her mom got to know my mom. And it was great! Especially so, because I was at the hospital when my mom was living in Arkansas, and my grandfather lived out of town from the hospital, so he couldn't be there every day. Most of the time, it was just me and my dear friend.

And when it wasn't, it ended up being my Uncle Keith who was there for me.

Those two showed up for me.

I haven't always gotten friendship right since then, but I keep them in the back of my mind to live by their examples. The two of them taught me to recognize who shows up for me when times are hard. Who shows up for me when I don't have the energy to show up for myself?

My goddaughter's mom and my Uncle Keith showed up for me, even when I didn't have the strength to show up for myself.

And yes, I chose the song *Girl* by Destiny's Child for this chapter, so sorry, Uncle Keith, but you're a #girldad and I know you get it. Thank you for that!

CHAPTER SIX

"When You Believe"
(Mariah Carey & Whitney Houston)

There's a song by Mariah Carey and Whitney Houston that I love called *When You Believe*, and the lyrics go like this:

"There can be miracles

when you believe ... In this

time of fear ... Yet now I'm

standing here."

Around the 5th grade, my grandmother got really sick. She was in the hospital in Kokomo, Indiana. They called all the family. My Uncle Keith ended up calling my grandfather, letting him know that they had been told she was about to die, and that we all needed to get to the hospital.

We all came. And eventually, we were all there together. All the kids. All the grandkids.

My grandmother told us, however, that God had told her that it wasn't her time yet. She didn't care what the doctors were telling her or us. She was good, she said, and she wasn't going anywhere. I have more time with you all, she informed us.

How Much Can I See?

The doctor, and I don't know if he was a non-believer or what, but my grandmother told him she didn't want him to be her doctor anymore.

"I'm telling you that God says it's not my time. I know that you study medicine," she told the doctor. "But I'm a child of the Lord, and he says it's not my time. It's not my time. And so, y'all can go home. I'm gonna be fine."

We indeed did have many more years of my grandmother after that. And I'm so thankful and so blessed to have experienced all that time with her.

But because of that experience that day in the hospital with her, I started to listen with more than my ears. And it was a wonderful new experience for me.

My grandmother never allowed doctors to tell her that they knew better than she did. She could tell when something wasn't right with her body, and she vocalized it. Consequently, she made me more confident in speaking up about the things that were ailing me.

Being a sick kid, I never wanted to draw attention, but at the same time, I always knew when there was a problem. I always knew when something was wrong with me. But, until that time, I was hesitant to voice my thoughts and concerns.

How Much Can I See?

So, back in 2005, after my grandmother had been in the hospital (and keep in mind that was the time shortly after my grandfather had picked me up from Arkansas and moved me back to Indiana, so I was not doing well emotionally), I got really sick again. And even though I was learning how to listen to what my body was telling me, it was hard for me to balance everything else happening around me.

My grandfather blamed my mom as the reason I was sick again. Mom was already hurting because she couldn't be there with me, and now she was being blamed for me being sick. I overheard an argument between them in which my grandfather told her that if she hadn't kept me in Arkansas, I wouldn't be sick.

It's sad to know that, at that time, I heard more arguments around me than comradery. Case in point, that Christmas, there was an argument. I'm not sure what all took place, but my grandmother had come to Indiana to bring me a snow globe and a stocking. My snow globe ended up getting busted, and the stocking was ruined because the globe was inside the stocking.

There was just a lot of drama, and I never could understand why they couldn't put that aside to support me. Why couldn't they look past their own issues to come together for me? I was a child. And I was dealing with a lot.

Sometimes, it felt like everyone always needed me to be strong for them, and yet, I was the sick child. I needed them to be there for me.

No one was ever strong for me, except for my Uncle Keith and my grandmother. No one else ever took the time to consider my feelings. Honestly, I don't remember anyone else even asking me about my feelings, until the Guardian ad Litem worked on my custody case.

When I was going to the blind school, we got out of school each day around 1:30 or 2 PM. On one particular day, my friend

Amber was coming to the house to stay for the weekend. But when we got to my house, I found out there was a guy named Mike waiting for me. And I was told he was my Guardian ad Litem, and that I needed to talk to him about why I wanted to go back to Arkansas and live with my mom.

One of the things I told him was that I wanted to get to know my brothers. He wasn't aware I had brothers. And it ended up being a turning point in the court case. Part of the reasoning given to the courts as to why I couldn't live with my mother was that she was an unfit mother. But then one of the questions became 'if she's so unfit then why don't you [meaning my grandfather] want both of her other children, too … why do you want just the one child?'

It was hard for me to learn as a kid that I was a burden, and with that burden came the question whether or not my family loved me and took care of me out of the kindness of their hearts or was it because I came with a disability check.

I think people forgot that I was still a child while all this was going on

Anyway, I talked to the Guardian ad Litem and told him I wanted to get to know my brothers. I wanted to know my family. And that meant that for now, I wanted to live in Arkansas.

It wasn't long after that we went back to court, and my mom won. But it was only for a trial basis. We had to check-in after six months to let them know how I was doing.

Having to go through the court and deal with that was a lot.

That said, for a period of time after that, I wanted to be a Guardian ad Litem because of how influential mine was in my life.

CHAPTER SEVEN

Arkansas Regrets

You know that whole thing about being careful what you wish for?

Well … living with my mom in Arkansas was really hard at times.

Traveling back to Arkansas from Indiana, I remember it was me, my mom, my oldest brother Miles, and my little brother, who we called Big Dante.

We really enjoyed the trip. I remember stopping to see my Uncle Keith in Indianapolis before leaving. And, after that, one of the fun things we did was we stopped in Memphis to catch a movie.

But I wasn't prepared for life in Arkansas.

I wasn't aware of a few key details.

There I was, finally in Arkansas, and I'm sitting in my room, in the dark, wondering if I had made the right decision.

For example, I wasn't aware that my little brother stole things, so some of the few nice things I had, I didn't have for long. Like my digital camera. A nice bracelet. I can't remember the third thing, but I didn't have a lot of nice items, so for those things to go missing was tough.

I was rather offhandedly that he steals. But I had never been in that situation before.

I was also only there for a week when our power got turned off for a few days. I had never experienced that before, either. Even though living with my grandfather and his wife was dysfunctional, the bills were paid. There was always food. And I never wondered what we were going to eat or that it would get too hot because there was no power. I never had to worry about that kind of stuff … until I lived with my mom.

And then, on top of that, I was afraid to report those things, fearful they would remove me from her home. And even though, she struggled, I wanted to be with her. So, I never said anything about those things happening.

I had only been there a couple of weeks when we had to move to a different house because there was an issue with the landlord. And that was an okay transition, because she made it that way, but it was just unexpected, and we started moving a lot those first couple of years.

It was really a crazy trip going from my grandfather's stability, which I don't think I appreciated until I didn't have it any longer.

How Much Can I See?

I had never experienced a time when I didn't have lights or food. I didn't know how much my mom was struggling to just stay afloat, but I sure did now.

I get that she wanted me, and I wanted to live with her more than anything, but as a child, I wasn't given the opportunity to know about these parts of her life before going there. That was a hard one to get used to.

For a while, I regretted moving in with her because of the instability. I hated not having lights sometimes, and that we had to move all the time. I didn't like that, at all.

But there were other things that happened in Arkansas that were fantastic! Like getting to go to Washington D. C. when

I was a sophomore – spending a week there with a couple of my classmates and one of our teachers. Such an incredible experience! We toured the capitol and all the monuments. So many people came through for me so that I could have that memory.

And then there was my grandmother ... I got to see her all the time.

Getting to know my brothers, even though our relationships were dysfunctional at times, was a treat!

I had a great eye doctor. And I got to speak at National Glaucoma Day a few times. I could really be immersed in the world of the visually impaired.

How Much Can I See?

Our church was really excellent. And getting to know the congregation was nice.

There were a lot of great things about living in Arkansas. But the things that were frustrating and terrible were really frustrating and really terrible.

CHAPTER EIGHT

"Chasing Cars"

(Snow Patrol)

I was a sophomore in high school when we got hit head on by another vehicle.

We were on my way to my grandmother's house. It was a Sunday night. It was my mother, my younger brother, and myself. We were at a four-way intersection, and this woman was fleeing a rough relationship, and the guy she was leaving fired a gun at her car, causing her to spin out of control. She crossed the line and hit us head on.

No one was seriously injured. However, I ended up in the hospital from a bad reaction to the pain meds they gave me.

But what messed me up was that, for a while, I was afraid of cars. I had so much anxiety about getting into a vehicle and about my mother driving. (Sometimes, I still have fears about my mom driving. She's been a couple of minor accidents since then.) It was terrifying to me, the realization that I could lose my mom, or my brother, or that it could have been worse than it was.

The woman who hit us ended up in the ambulance with me. And I can so clearly remember her crying a lot. She realized the car she had hit – our car – had children in it.

That's when I understood mortality, really got it, for the first time. I realized that I had survived a lot of things. Yeah, God had gotten me through a whole lot of things. Knowing that, I was still struggling with my Faith. I knew that God got me through, but the reality was I couldn't understand why I had to keep going through things. *Why did I continue to have to keep overcoming things?*

My Faith had been wavering for a while. Sometimes, I was very strong in my Faith, and you couldn't tell me anything otherwise. I knew that 'God has got me!' There were other times, though, when I was just like … 'Why? Why am going through this?' *Why do I have gall stones? Why do I have a bowel obstruction? Why can't I just live with my mom all the time?*

I never realized God was putting me through all those paces so I could be more prepared to be here today. More prepared to tell my story from a place of healing. From a place of having learned. A place of having experienced.

How Much Can I See?

At that time, I was just like 'Dang! Why, God?' *Have I not been through enough? Have I not suffered enough? Now you have to take our car?! You have to hurt me, my mom, my brother? You have to put me in the hospital again for a week?*

I was just tired! I was Just Tired!

But it was another moment that was a wake-up call. I saw things differently, despite my paranoia.

While my mom was saving up for a new car, there was a period of time she took the bus to her job. And I remember being even more paranoid if she didn't come home right away, that maybe she couldn't get a ride, or she had missed the bus and was stranded somewhere. I worried more about things after that accident than I had ever worried about anything in my life. My Faith waivered so much. I was just never really sure about anything for a long while. Was my mom going to make it home safely? Was I going to make it home safely?

I was so uncertain about a whole lot of things. And that's a hard thing to acknowledge. It was just like, 'Damn! I don't know what's going to happen today or tomorrow.' And how do I accept that? How do I accept that I don't know and just continue to move forward? That's a strength I prayed for every day.

How Much Can I See?

Interestingly enough, it's the kind of strength my grandmother had. She had this amazing ability to not know what was going to happen to her tomorrow, but to know that God was going to take her there and through it.

M. L. Farrell

CHAPTER NINE
My Mom's Strength

One of the things that took place in Arkansas, as I mentioned previously, was the car accident. The accident took place right before Thanksgiving, so I had been in Arkansas around six months. We had a decent house then, and things seemed to be okay.

That was also a period of time where I got to see how strong my mom really was. I witnessed her, even though it was hard, save money for a new car. Until then, she took the bus, or she caught a ride from a coworker, or called a cab. She did whatever she needed to do to get from Point A to B to get to work.

I'm completely blessed that God gifted me with the strength of my mother. There have been so many times in life that I would have given up, and I wanted to give up, and for my mom, I imagine that there were many times as a single mom that she wanted to do the same. She was a single mom of three. She had me, a sick kid with a disability. She had a kid who was acting out and stealing. And a kid who was discovering his sexuality.

My mom was dealing with a lot, but she did it with a lot of poise and grace.

My mom wasn't perfect by any means, but she did the best she could, and I really know that. She really tried for us. She tried to make sure that we were okay. She tried to make sure she supported us in whatever activities we wanted to do.

She tried, but she struggled. And because she struggled, she instilled in us the willingness to keep trying; that if we kept trying, we'd be okay.

I think it took a while for my mom to find her rhythm and her overall comfort zone, but when she found it, we were really okay.

We were okay. And we were loved.

My mom's goal was to be a good mother and a good daughter. And she did the best she could to be that.

She had her first kid when she was 19, during her first semester of college. She had to grow up while raising her children.

My mother had a lot working against her for a while, but her strength has been one of the best resources for my own strength, and I'll be forever blessed and grateful to her for that.

CHAPTER TEN

"Grey's Anatomy"

When I think about moments in my life that shaped the person I am today, one moment really stands out. I was a senior in high school back in 2009, and I had decided over the summer that I wanted to graduate from public school, even though I was doing well at the blind school in Arkansas. Things were good, but I didn't want to graduate from the blind school. I wanted the public-school experience. And I still had enough vision to do so.

I went to the blind school administration and asked them if I could take Math and English at the blind school and go to public school the rest of the day. There was another kid who was being allowed to do that for his senior year. He took a couple of classes at the blind school and then he went back to his own high school. I was ultimately told 'No' I couldn't do that, so I ended up enrolling in public school full-time.

I was doing pretty well up until December…

How Much Can I See?

I went to a party with this girl, after the winter formal, and someone slipped something into my drink.

I don't really remember much after that. I made it home. I remember hanging out a while with my brother. But then I got sick, and I stayed sick for a while, waking up one day with this really weird rash. Something told me that I was pregnant, but I was having a really hard time believing that I could be pregnant. *This can't be happening to me. I'm only a senior.*

I went to the doctor, and of course because I was 18, they ran a pregnancy test. They came back in and told me that the test was positive and that I had some weird pregnancy. The rash was a strange pregnancy thing.

Ultimately, at that time, I was not ready to support a child. So, my mom and I decided to keep it very under wraps, and she took me for an abortion.

Aside from the trauma of that experience on its own, they had to wake me up during the procedure because I wasn't reacting well to the anesthesia. So, I was alert part of the time, and in a lot of pain. It was a really big deal.

I remember I was so miserable because, due to the anesthesia, I was coming in and out of consciousness. I was dizzy and so uncomfortable. It was bad.

How Much Can I See?

And it was a hard thing to recover from. I spotted consistently for about a week. I was just miserable. I thought my health would get better after that, but it really, really took a turn for the worst. They had told me that I could have a bunch of health problems that could occur after the abortion, but they couldn't figure out what was wrong with me and what was causing so much abdominal pain.

I started missing a lot of school. We were trying to work with the teachers and let them know that I was very sick. And so, the teachers decided to give me a computer so that I could do the homework at home. I only had three classes left to graduate, and they were willing to work with me.

I got the computer. And I remember the day I got it, we ended up having to take my grandmother to the hospital because she was having chest pain. At the time, we thought she was having a heart attack, and it was terrifying because of the fact that both of her parents had lost their lives to a heart attack.

So, we all showed up at the hospital, and part of the reason I remember that day is because I had been sick for so long after my abortion, and when I showed up at the hospital with my mom, my grandmother was shocked to see me.

How Much Can I See?

"What is Michele doing here?" she asked. "Every time she goes to the hospital, they try to keep her."

"If they tried to keep me, I would just ask them to put me in the room with you because I am 18 now," I said.

And that made us all laugh.

It must have been the last week of April that year. And I just couldn't move. By that time, I had a catheter because I couldn't walk well enough to get to the bathroom. I couldn't be home alone any longer, either, because I was so unstable, I'd fallen down the stairs. On this particular day, I was on the phone with my best friend, and we were just having a casual conversation, when all of a sudden, I felt really, really dizzy. I told her not to freak out, but that I thought I was going to die. I remember it was a weekend, and my little brother was home. I told him we needed to call 911 and one of us also needed to call our mom.

Something was really wrong, and I needed to go to the hospital.

The EMTs showed up, and they took my blood pressure, and it was like 220 over 159. It was so high that it was legitimately terrifying. They thought I was having a stroke. The ambulance would only take me so far, to North Little Rock. We lived in Jacksonville, at the time. My mom wanted me to go to Baptist, which was in Little

Rock. She asked me if I could hold on long enough to get there. And I did.

At Baptist Health, we spent hours in the Emergency Room, until I finally got a room. I was in so much pain. And my blood pressure was so high, there was no way they could send me home, even though they didn't know what was wrong with me.

For a week, they did x-rays and tests. Everything they could possibly do, they did. One day, they decided to test me for gall stones. My stomach was so distended, and I was in so much pain, that even doing the ultrasound made me miserable. But it had to be done.

The technician revealed that I did have a lot of gall stones. It was horrible, so they took me for a gall bladder test, using some sort of purple liquid. And the test showed that my gall bladder was not in good shape, at all.

So, I had another surgery, and my gall bladder was removed. Four days later, I was able to go home.

The issue now was that I had missed so much school, and my school wasn't willing to give me another computer, which meant I ended up not graduating that year. It would be four more years before I would graduate from high school. The reason being my brother stole the laptop the public school gave me the first go-round to support his marijuana habit. He did that a lot. He stole a lot of things. But that was one of the things he did that would change our relationship for perhaps the rest of our lives.

I didn't officially get my diploma till 2014. And that's crazy! I'm still considered an alumni at the public school I went to and the blind school. As far as they're concerned, I graduated in 2010, but I'm still really embarrassed that I didn't officially graduate. That's a truth that really hurts.

When people ask me when I graduated, I still say 2010, and I know that's technically a lie, but I claim that because that's my truth. I worked hard to graduate in 2010. I don't care that technically I had three classes left that I couldn't finish until 2014. I didn't drop out of school. I didn't do anything wrong. It was a medical thing that kept me from graduating and the ignorance of one person, the selfishness of one person that shaped my life.

CHAPTER ELEVEN

"A New Day Has Come"
(Celine Deion)

I think that one of the best moments of my life actually happened when I made the choice to go to Indypendence Job Corps in Downtown Indianapolis. I had made the choice in 2013 that I was going to do it, because I was tired of not being able to get a job that was meaningful and could provide me with some longevity and security.

I knew that part of the problem was that I hadn't finished my schooling. I didn't have a diploma to provide a prospective employer. So, around October 2013, my mom and I were going to get me some new glasses, and I heard an advertisement on the radio for Job Corps. I thought this might be cool for me to do. *I'm going to try it!*

I put the number in my phone and contacted them. They had a meeting with me in their office where they gave me lots of information and told me that even though they'd never had someone with a disability come through their program, they would help me as much as they could.

I got in touch with Vocational Rehab in Indianapolis, and they said they'd also help make this happen for me.

At the time, though, I started getting sick again, and had to put it all on the backburner. I was sick for months! I ended up in the hospital for a few months, and it took me a long time to recover from that. I couldn't start the program until June 2014.

However, when I was able to start, they did exactly what they said they would. I had all my accommodations. The teachers were really understanding, and it was great! I had a lot of support, especially from a teacher named Mrs. Reynolds. Another teacher, Miss Milton. And, it was just great, a great experience! I also met a lot of young girls with major challenges.

They gave me this test to see where I was in my schooling – to see, for example, if I needed help in Math or English or something else. I took the test with accommodations, meaning I got extra time to take it, and someone read the test to me. After the scores came in, they pulled me aside.

"What's wrong?" I asked, horrified that something was going to prevent me from finishing the program and securing a job.

How Much Can I See?

"Maya, you got the highest scores that we've seen in a really … really … long time."

They then asked me why I didn't graduate. I told them about my brother and the computer situation, and they understood and, because my scores were off the charts, they offered to get me what I needed to finish. Most people, they explained, needed to take remedial classes, but since I didn't need that, they were going to get me in and out, so I could finish quickly. I finished the high school diploma class in less than two weeks, and I chose Office Administration as my trade. I completed everything in six months.

By the time Christmas rolled around, I was already doing job interviews, and by the time I graduated, I had a job offer at Lowe's Companies in their call center.

I was supposed to start with them the following February, but it took awhile for them to get my system working with all the extra tech I needed for visually impaired accommodations. Enter their IT Guy, Seth, who I mentioned previously! He was so understanding and did everything he could to make my transition a smooth one. Any time I needed him, he was right there for me. He supported me in a way that was awesome!

How Much Can I See?

I didn't feel bad about myself anymore. I didn't feel like an inconvenience.

Lowe's was very understanding. The first training class they put me in didn't work out. So, they ended up putting me in the class again, which was great. I learned, over time, how to be effective in my job. And I kept that job for five years.

I had a couple of health incidents while I was there – one in 2016 (I had a major hernia repair) and then one in 2017 (I had some chronic pain issues and a couple eye surgeries). They were just really understanding. Ultimately, I left the job because of my chronic pain around 2020. In addition, my vision loss was becoming more acute. It was no longer healthy for me to work on a computer, day to day.

That was something that shaped me. It helped me believe that I can go somewhere and get a job and be the first person in that industry or place of employment to do so and pave the way for other people with disabilities. By the time I left Lowe's, there were a couple of other people who had visual impairments who were working successfully for them, and they were happy there, too. I paved the way for them. The IT Department knew how to use the tech we needed and how to help us do our jobs.

CHAPTER TWELVE

"Take Me to the King"
(Tamela Mann)
A Conversation About Faith

It was weird because growing up in my grandfather's house, there was no Faith, there was no going to church. Nothing like that. But any time I went to see my grandmother, my mom and my family, I knew I would be going to church.

I would see my cousins at church — church was where we went on the weekends to see our family.

But still, as a child, I didn't understand because I wasn't exposed to religion regularly. In Arkansas, being a part of a church felt forced to me. For the most, by then, I had spent the better part of ten years outside the church.

Once I got old enough to not go, about 17, I stopped going, especially because, by that time, we didn't live in the same city as my grandmother, so we didn't always have a ride to church.

It was sad because I only prayed when something was wrong with my health.

When the doctor told me I was having another surgery, for example. Like most sinners, that's when I would start praying again. And it was like that for a while.

Moving back to Indiana, it took us a while to find a church. Then, I found one, but we didn't go consistently, so … you know, my relationship with God was one that wasn't stable.

But then in 2016, I had another major surgery. And I was tired. I was so tired of being sick. This is also when my relationship with my ex really began to change. So, I started praying more and reading the Bible and becoming familiar with Faith. And it was then that I realized I had a partner who wouldn't pray with me.

I was at a point where they couldn't figure out what was wrong with me health wise, so all I had was God. So, I really connected with Him. And I realized I was happier when I prayed, when I truly believed … when I let go and let God.

Even though I have struggled off and on with my Faith, I have maintained that relationship. I do daily devotionals now, I pray, I try to surround myself with people I feel comfortable talking to about my religion. I had been in a relationship with someone who was suppressing that part of me. And I finally realized it was so unhealthy.

Now, Faith is such an integral part of me, and my belief is such an integral part of me. Having friends I can pray with is so very important to me.

But I had to grow to get here. I really had to grow. I had to focus on my spirit, and once I started healing my spirit, I was more open to therapies, and I could heal my mind, body, and soul – heal from having a miscarriage, from losing my grandmother, from losing the dog I'd had since I was 13. My ex's brother died, and then a guy I was dating died. It was just a lot of death and a lot of pain. And if I didn't have the relationship I did with God, I would have given up.

2018 was hard. I had left my ex in June. A couple of weeks later, I found out I was pregnant. And then I miscarried. The miscarriage was insane. Inside of it being traumatic, it was hard because my ex was suicidal, and he was attempting to kill himself. Also, my grandmother was in the hospital in Arkansas after visiting us all for six weeks in Indiana. And then, she was in a nursing home for a while.

It was just so rocky there for a long while.

I didn't really get to deal with the miscarriage as my grandmother died a couple of months after it. Her health had been steadily declining, and I needed to focus on that. And then, my dog died, a few days after my birthday in 2019. Then, my ex's brother had Muscular Dystrophy, and he died in March 2019. A guy I was starting to talk to had Sickle Cell Anemia, and he also died in March 2019.

While all this was going on, I was also was having issues with my sinuses. During that time, I was afraid I was going to die during the surgery I needed for that. I kept telling everyone I wasn't confident about the procedure.

I ended up in ICU after waking up from that surgery, so when I started healing from that, I was due for another eye surgery, and while I was healing from that, I began having problems with my ovaries.

I could not win! By the time 2020 came around, trauma, after trauma, after trauma, for the last 18 months … damn, I was ready to give up.

There was talk about removing my ovaries, and then it got cancelled at the last minute because it was determined to be an unsafe procedure for me. I dealt with that for months while also dealing with declining vision.

If I didn't have my Faith, if I didn't have people praying for me – as I was at the point, I didn't even want to pray for myself anymore – I don't even want to think what would have happened.

I had people praying for me, praying with me and over me. And I was able to not just bounce back but to bounce back better than ever.

Even having to make the choice to leave my job (because it was causing more damage to my vision) wasn't as traumatic because I had my Faith. I knew I was going to be fine. I knew that God was going to take care of me.

So, that's why Faith is so important, and why I am the way I am. Why I will pray first, before anything. I will now let things go and really give them to God because He is the end all to be all, and without Him, none of us would be here.

CHAPTER THIRTEEN

"Beautiful"
(Christina Aguilera)
Setting My Value

Growing up with a disability, one of the hardest parts is trying to date.

I think, as a joke or a dare, I kissed a boy in the 3rd grade, but in the 5th grade, I remember really liking this kid named Caleb. But I was a kid, and I didn't really know what it was like to have a boyfriend.

Part of that relationship was about making me feel that I wasn't less than all the other girls.

It was a while before I really liked someone after that, but eventually I did, and his name was Avery. I met him during summer camp at blind school. I liked him sooo so much. We used to talk on the phone and do the other things that many kids did, but it was just a summer camp thing until I actually was going to the blind school full-time. After which, we dated off and on for a little over a year. It was such a great time and good relationship.

It was weird to have boys like me in that structured place at blind school. It didn't matter that it was blind boys. It just mattered that there were boys finally paying attention to me. I didn't realize how much I needed that until I received it.

I don't want to say I was fast. That's a strong statement. But I did like boys. And yeah, I went through a phase where I liked them a lot!

Then, when I left for Arkansas, boys liked me a lot there, too.

It took a while, maybe when I was 16 or so, before I thought I was actually pretty. I didn't believe it. I thought people told me that I was beautiful to be polite. I didn't start to believe it until boys starting to show they liked me. That was when I first had self-worth … because boys liked me.

I dated the same guy for a couple of years, and his name was Erick. We dated as teenagers do, so he did some wrong, and I did some wrong. He was one of the last people I dated for a while. But, I still talked to a lot of guys.

What was interesting was that when I moved back to Indiana in 2012, I met my ex – Marquis – and there were times in that relationship that were really good, but we didn't start in a healthy way, and neither did we end in a healthy way. We both came from broken homes, raised by single moms.

How Much Can I See?

That said, one of the hardest things about him was that he never made me feel like I was enough.

It took me a while after being with him to feel like I was in fact enough. It took me time to realize I had to stop allowing other people to control my value. I had to stop allowing others to set my value. I had to set value for myself.

That was a big, Big part of my dating life.

After I stopped dated Marquis, I was finally able to value myself and have my own self-worth.

CHAPTER FOURTEEN

"Never Would Have Made It"
(Marvin Sapp)
The Safety of Suicide

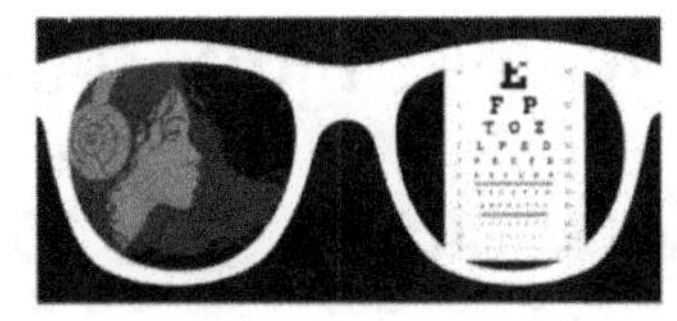

I've talked about being in a dark place because of my health, but there are two times in my life where I've considered suicide …

The first was when my grandfather came to Arkansas and brought the cop saying my mom kidnapped me. I thought my mom was going to go to jail. I was 13, and I didn't know any better. All I could think about was that if she was in jail, I couldn't live with her, and I didn't want to go back to Indiana.

All I thought about that entire car ride was that I wanted to die. I just didn't want to live anymore. I was tired of going back and forth. I was tired of my family fighting. I didn't have a relationship with any of them, really. What I had was a disability. And I was just really, really lonely and tired of it all.

I was alone – I don't know how to even begin describing how lonely it feels to be visually impaired. All I could think about was committing suicide and just being done with all of it.

The other time I considered suicide was in 2020, when the darkness of the 18 months from mid-2018 to the beginning of 2020 were just too much for me. I was in so much pain due to my ovaries. I didn't have a great pain doctor. There was a period of time then that I simply did not want to live anymore.

What am I living for? What is the purpose I get up every day? Why carry the constant pain?

It took so much prayer, so much truth to face of my own, to say it's worth it to live, to be alive, to not shut people out, that it's worth it to be here.

All I had ever wanted to do was inspire people.

How could I do that if I gave up?

I decided I needed to expose the darkness.

I made the choice to expose my darkness.

It may seem like it takes a lot for me to share so much light with the world and so much love, given my life history. But the truth is that I've only been able to show that kind of strength because I've also been able to show my pain … and speak of my darkness. That's my truth. That's my story.

How Much Can I See?

I thought, in my darkest days, that suicide could offer me the safety I craved. There was safety in suicide for me, at least that's what I thought it would offer me.

Living with a disability isn't about living with just one disability. Most people who live with a disability, like me, have multiple disabilities. There's darkness upon darkness. My blindness, for example, is but one part of my health issues. From cancer to gall stones to high blood pressure, chronic pain, ovarian cysts, and sinus problems, my life, if I'm focused on all that, is a very dark place. I've been there. I've struggled. And I've wanted to give up, too. That's a very natural reaction.

People always say that God never gives us more than we can handle, and I know that logically, that's true, but emotionally, why should I have had to handle so much?

How did I find the strength to seek safety somewhere else rather than in suicide?

I'm still figuring all that out, but I'm so glad I chose to stay here and find the answers I'm seeking.

Epilogue

"Wings"
(Little Mix)
Rain Drops Make Puddles

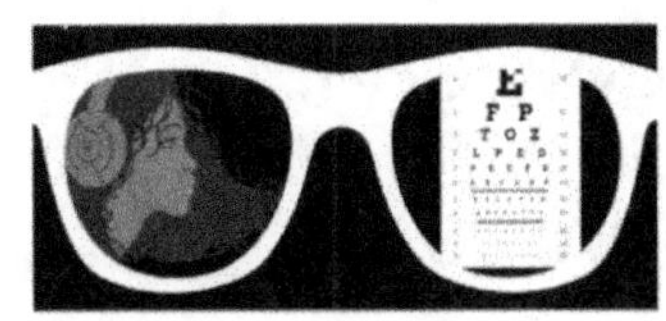

Now that I'm on my way to healing, it's important to me for my family, and each of you reading this, to understand some of my pain. I don't have to put on a front anymore. It took me a long time to be able to be emotionally vulnerable and emotionally available. I lived so long without being able to do that. But I will live that way no more.

All these things I've shared with you have shaped me as an adult.

The little things. The big things. And all the things in between.

It's like raindrops …

One raindrop doesn't make a puddle, but millions of raindrops do.

And depending on the circumstances, whether it's a sprinkle or an all-out deluge, you never know how deep that puddle is going to be.

Depending on how deep that puddle is going to determine how long it takes for it to dry out. For that water to evaporate. For that solid ground to show again.

I'm back on solid ground now. All dried off. The sun is shining. And I'm ready for the next chapter in my life. I'm ready to spread my wings like a butterfly.

The question is:

How Much Can I See ...

now that I've come out of

the darkness?

ACKNOWLEDGEMENTS

I am truly blessed and thankful to God for reaching this goal. I have so much love and appreciation for all my family and friends who have shown me their love and support. Special thank you to my parents and my siblings, both the natural and chosen ones. I love you all. To my readers, again, I thank you all and look forward to sharing more with you.

NOTE FROM THE AUTHOR

I would like to take time to thank everyone who has followed my journey as a person and as an author. I have survived so much, and I want you all to know that I take nothing for granted.

This is my first book, and I hope you will all follow me on my journey to see what comes next. And please leave a review so that other people can discover my books as well.

I would also love to connect with you at:

Facebook: Michele Farrell

Instagram: @MsCapricorn92

Twitter: @MsCapricorn92

Clubhouse

ABOUT THE AUTHOR

M. L. Farrell is a native of Indiana, although she did reside in Arkansas for several years and has some beloved family still living there. She attended The School for the Blind and Visually-Impaired in

Indiana as well as in Arkansas. She also received her Certification in Office Administration through Indypendence Job Corp. She has faced several health challenges head on, and it is her hope that through her writing you feel strengthened and inspired, as well as entertained.

BOOKS BY M. L. FARRELL

HOW MUCH CAN I SEE?

(A Novel in Essays) – Volume I

More Coming Soon!